D1643563

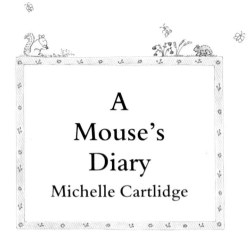

A Mouse's Diary
Michelle Cartlidge

Also by Michelle Cartlidge

The Bears' Bazaar
Gerry's Seaside Journey

First published in 1981
Miniature edition first published 1993
by William Heinemann Ltd
an imprint of Reed Consumer Books Limited
Michelin House, 81 Fulham Road, London SW3 6RB
and Auckland, Melbourne, Singapore and Toronto

0 434 96386 0

Produced by Mandarin
Printed and bound in Singapore

My Diary
Mousefield School
Summer Term

Sunday

I went to the park with my father and
mother and younger brother. We had a
lovely picnic. Some tiny birds hopped
up to us, wanting something to eat,
and we fed them crumbs of bread. My
brother tried to catch one, but he
couldn't. They just flew away.

Monday

At ballet class today we pretended to be candles on a great big birthday cake. The teacher said we looked more like scarecrows than pretty candles. In the middle of the dancing I had to stop and change over my ballet shoes because they were on the wrong feet.

Tuesday

After school my mother took us to the toy shop. First I wanted to buy the pink elephant. Then I saw the dolls' furniture and I chose a chair and a wardrobe for my dolls' house. My brother bought a little wooden train. We spent all our pocket money.

Wednesday

The whole class went out on a Nature
Find. We saw squirrels high up in the
trees. We found leaves of different
shapes and colours. I saw some tiny
frogs and tried to catch butterflies.
Back at school we labelled everything
for our Nature Table.

Thursday

My brother and I played dressing up.
He was a Viking and I was a smart
lady in a long silky dress. I put on lots
of red lipstick. Then my brother
dressed up as a ghost. He made
horrible noises, but I wasn't
frightened. My mother wasn't very
pleased when she saw all the mess we
had made.

Friday

While we were playing
in the street, we saw a
big removal van outside
one of the houses. We
watched all the furniture
being loaded into the van.
The removal mice were very
careful not to drop anything. We
giggled when we noticed other mice
peering out of their windows to see
what was going on.

MOUSE MOVES

RADIO CONTROLLED

VANS

Saturday

My best friend came to play. She lives
next door to me and we sit next to
each other in class. It rained all day, so
my mother took us to the cake shop for
a treat. I had a large creamy cake with
a cherry on top and my friend had a
chocolate one.

Sunday

On Sunday mornings my parents like reading the newspapers, so we have to keep out of their way. We had a smashing pillow fight. I was squashed flat on the floor. There were feathers flying everywhere. My naughty brother ripped a pillow by mistake and we had a lot of clearing up to do.

Monday

My best friend came again today.
I showed her my new dolls' furniture
and we played with my dolls' house.
We put two dollies upstairs in bed
ready for their goodnight story, and
one dolly in front of the mirror. Then
I put two more dollies in the kitchen
to have their supper. We sat the other
two in armchairs by the fire.

Tuesday

The whole class went to the library for story time. We heard about an elephant that runs away from the jungle and meets a very rich old lady who lives in the town. Then we all chose books to look at. I pulled one off the shelf and a whole lot fell down with a big bang on the floor. We are supposed to be very quiet in the library.

Wednesday

Today a postcard came from my granny. We are going to tea with her on Saturday. After school we went to the pond, because my brother wanted to feed the ducks. They were very hungry and kept on quacking for more. We saw some fluffy yellow ducklings far across the pond. They swam to meet us too.

Thursday

Tomorrow is the last day of term and we are having a Punch and Judy show and a party tea. Today our teacher showed us how to make place mats and hats out of crepe paper for the party. My best friend and I tried on our hats to see how they looked. I'm so excited, I can't wait until tomorrow.

Friday

The Punch and Judy show came today.
There was a little brown dog called
Toby, who did lots of funny tricks. He
even did a dance for us. Mr Punch was
naughty and held his baby upside
down. We were all frightened when the
crocodile came out from under the
curtain and growled. Then
we had our party tea and
wore our paper hats.

Saturday

Today we went to see Granny and I told her all about the party and the Punch and Judy show. Then my brother and I played hide and seek around her plants, peeping at each other through the leaves. We knocked over one of the best plants, and poor Granny was very upset. We said we were sorry and would be more careful next time.

Sunday

Now I have filled up my diary, I am
going to read it to my toys for their
special goodnight story.